D1075416

Library of Congress Catalog Card Number: 00-100899
Printed in the United States of America   October 2000   10 9 8 7 6 5 4 3
RANDOM HOUSE and colophon are registered trademarks of Random House, Inc.

Now It's Fall

LOIS LENSKI

Random House New York

Summer's over,
   Now it's fall;
Just the nicest
   Time of all.

Down,
    down,
        down,
Leaves of red and gold and brown
    Come falling,
        falling
            down.

Now the wind says,
  "Come and play!"
Catch them if you can—
  Hooray!

Rustle, scuffle,
Kick them
With your toe.
Scuffle, bustle,
Kick them
As you go.

See all we've found
Down on the ground!
Let's rake awhile
And make a big pile.

Down under the leaves
 In the pile I go.
Cover me up
 From head to toe!

Rain, rain,
   On the windowpane!
Softly it taps and taps again.
Rain, rain,
   On the windowpane.

We like to walk in the rain,
    In the rain,
    In the rain,
Until the sun comes out again.

Apples are ripe
  In the fall.
Let's climb the ladder
  And pick them all.

Oh, what a load!
   We must tug and pull.
The basket is heavy
   When it is full.

Nuts are falling
　　From the trees.
We go picking
　　On our knees.
Squirrels, too,
　　Come and play,
Pick up nuts,
　　And run away.

Ding, dong! Oh, what fun!
The school bell rings,
   School's begun.
Boys and girls, hurry away,
Back to school again today.

It's fun to go to school,
To read and write and spell.

It's fun to go to school—
I like it very well.

Fly away to the south,
 Little birds, fly away.
Fly back again to us
 On a warm spring day.

Great big golden pumpkins
Ripen in the fall.
From the kitchen garden
We will bring them all.

Oh, see!
What fun it will be—
Make a pumpkin face
   With nose and eyes,
Mouth wide open
   In surprise!

Oooh, oooh!
It's scary, too,
When the light
Shines out at night!

Let's cut out witches
    And big black cats;
And then we'll make
    Some pointed hats.

Sister's a witch
    With broom and hat.
How funny she looks
    Dressed like that!
Ha, ha! Ho, ho! Hee, hee!
    She's just as funny
    As she can be.

We all wear masks for Halloween—
Funniest faces ever seen!

Ha, ha! Ho, ho! Hee, hee!
We're just as funny as we can be!

Gobble, gobble, turkey,
  Run while you can,
Or someone will catch you
  And put you in a pan!

We thank Thee, Lord,
  For gifts of food;
For sunshine, health,
  And every good.
Our very special thanks we say
  On this Thanksgiving Day.

Down,
  down,
    down,
Leaves of red and gold and brown
        Come falling,
            falling
              down.

Summer's over,
Now it's fall;
Just the nicest
Time of all.